THE OFFICIAL
Five Nights at Freddy's™
HOW TO DRAW

SCHOLASTIC INC.

CONTENTS

HELLO?...HELLO?

While these animatronics are often seen in dynamic, action-filled poses, don't worry: if you follow the step-by-step guides closely, you will be able to draw them in no time. These instructions will take you from rough stick figures to fully detailed drawings of all your favorite cast members.

Take care when drawing these characters. They don't often look at you head-on. They like to stand at angles. This will challenge what artists call "perspective." It means some body parts that are tilted away from you will look smaller than those parts that are closer to you. This might take a bit of practice to get right, so be patient and keep trying.

Every animatronic can be broken down into simple shapes. Try warming up by sketching rectangles, circles, cubes, and cylinders. And remember: keep your pencil lines light. That way, it's easy to erase any rough workings to get your drawings just right.

Smooth plain paper, a good hard black pencil, and an eraser are essential tools for getting started. Soft black pencils are great for shading, but don't worry if you don't have a variety of pencils. Just one pencil can create a huge range of tones by varying the pressure applied. Keep a ruler and pencil sharpener on standby.

Finally, the instructions provided in this book are a guide to help you. Don't be afraid to experiment with the animatronics and position them in different poses. Just don't get too close when night falls . . .

Have fun—and don't give up!

FREDDY

Drawing Freddy Fazbear is easy! Keep his features soft and friendly. Don't forget to add a bright shine to his eyes.

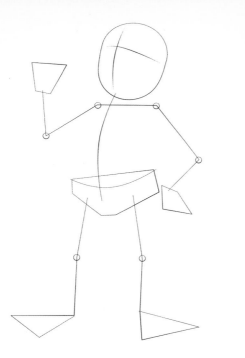

1 Begin by lightly sketching Freddy's framework, keeping his stance wide. Add guidelines for his facial features, noting the tilted angle of his face.

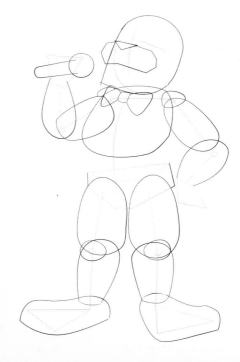

2 Add shape to his body, leaving space between your frame and outline to capture his broad limbs. Sketch his bow tie, muzzle, and microphone.

3 Use simple shapes to add his top hat, eyes, and ears. Curl his fingers around the microphone and use curved lines to outline his toes.

4 Start adding detail to your drawing, defining the shape of Freddy's jaw. Mark the animatronic joints on his body at his ears, knees, and elbows.

5 Firm up your outline and erase any guidelines. Mark sections of highlights where the spotlight will hit Freddy's top hat and bow tie.

6 Darkly shade Freddy's accessories and the mechanical bends on his body. Add a few soft lines to your drawing to create a rough texture.

BONNIE

This "hare"-raisin' rabbit loves to rock out on his guitar. Take care when drawing his fingers to make sure he hits the right notes!

1

Create Bonnie's framework. He's a confident performer, so keep his stance wide and emphasize the bends at the elbows, ready to hold his guitar.

2

Begin adding form to your framework. Although parts of Bonnie will be covered in the final drawing, it is useful to sketch his full body to ensure proportions are correct.

3

Outline Bonnie's eyes, muzzle, bow tie, hands, and ears. His articulated ears are raised slightly above his head, so remember to leave a small gap for the hinges.

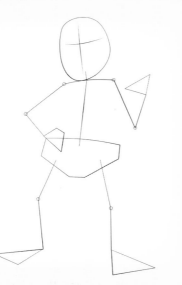

4

Pencil in the guitar's frame. Start with a long straight line for the neck, topping it with a triangle. A rhomboid creates the body's main shape.

5 Continue building the guitar's shape, curling Bonnie's fingers around the neck. Add a curl to the tip of his ears and open his jaw. Outline his toes.

6 Start adding detail to Bonnie's face. Draw his rounded teeth and use small circles for his big, bright pupils. Add shape to his fingers and details to his guitar.

7 Firm up your outline and erase any rough line work. Add strings to the guitar and lightly shade Bonnie's eyes, jaw, and hinges on his body.

8 Finish by shading the darkest areas of your drawing, keeping Bonnie's body and the colorful parts of his guitar a bright white.

CHICA

Chica is the bird who likes to eat! She is never without Mr. Cupcake.

1

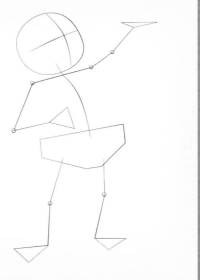

Sketch Chica's frame, with a round head and wide pelvis. As her left arm is stretched high, the lines forming her raised arm will be slightly shorter than those on the right.

2

Add shape to Chica's body, curving the outline away from her frame, with an emphasis on the bend in her torso to show the upward tilt in her stance.

3

Carefully use your guidelines to add her facial features. Mark a tuft of feathers on her head, falling in curved sections, and outline her hands.

4

Draw a circle for the shape of Mr. Cupcake, with smaller circles within for his eyes. Add a candle, and a thin plate on Chica's hand.

5

Place Chica's bib on her torso, following the shape of her body. Sketch her fingers and talons. Draw her eyebrows and large pupils, keeping the angle of her head in mind.

6

Decorate Chica's bib with bubble letters. Draw both characters' teeth, leaving a gap in Chica's grin. Use circles to add a glint to their eyes.

ART TIP

Semicircles with lightly curved bases create Chica's talons. Practice drawing them at different angles.

7

Erase any remaining guidelines. Add a few short lines to Chica's body to capture her worn texture. Define Mr. Cupcake's dripping icing with a wavy line.

8

Firm up your linework and use thick blacks to shade Chica's eyebrows and mechanical hinges, and the characters' sockets.

FOXY

This stealthy pirate moves quickly. Identify his lines of action before you start drawing to bring his running pose to life.

1

Pencil in Foxy's framework. Exaggerate his stance, with his limbs bending dramatically, to create a sense of movement in your drawing.

2

Flesh out the plated areas of his body, leaving his lower legs bare. Foxy's torso is squarer than the other animatronics'.

3

Mark his facial features, with his snout just below his eyeline. Outline his ears. Pencil in his hook, slim calves, and rectangular feet.

4

Use curved lines for his hair and the rough metal on his shoulders. Mark his fingers and refine his hook. Turn his raised foot into a cuboid to create a 3D look.

5 Draw Foxy's eyes and eyebrows. Give him sharp cone-shaped teeth, leaving small gaps between those on his bottom jaw. Define his inner ear and his robotic fingers.

6 Outline his damaged areas and raised eye patch. Finish shaping his feet, breaking the sections down into squares and rectangles.

7 Erase any remaining guidelines. Add short lines to his hook, giving it a 3D look. Begin adding value to the darkest areas of your drawing.

ART TIP
The direction of a character's gaze can help to convey movement. Ensure Foxy is looking where he is going.

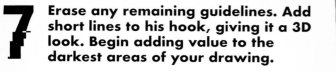

8 Refine your pencil work and darkly shade Foxy's tears. Leave thin white highlights on his nose and eye patch to emphasize their curved shape.

CIRCUS BABY

Drawing Baby may look hard, but don't let her trick you. Take your time with her outline and the rest will fall into place.

1

Pencil in Circus Baby's framework. Her pose will challenge perspective. Notice the light curve in her spine and the tilt of her head as she looks toward her audience.

2

Add shape to her limbs, drawing ovals for her arms and legs, with the curves tapering around her joints to emphasize the bend in her right knee. Use small circles for her kneecaps.

3

Curl the toes of her shoes to resemble jester boots. Place her facial features, with her nose slightly curved at the tip. Sketch two large circles to place her pigtails, and outline the palms of her hands.

4

Curved lines create her fingers and eyelashes. Draw small circles for her rosy cheeks, the bells on her shoes, the fan in her stomach, and the pins in her limbs. Add her frilly skirt and sleeves.

5 Draw her pigtails, following the curve of the circles closely. Add her bangs and her small, square teeth. Two circles and a long rectangle form her microphone.

6 Sketch the panels on Circus Baby's limbs, and curved lines for the soles of her boots. Stack cylinders to form her fingers and add her small fan.

7 Erase any remaining guidelines and tidy your line work. Add light lines around her skirt to give the metal a softer, fabric-like appearance.

8 Contrast a thick outline with light lines within Circus Baby's body to highlight her segmented plates.

MANGLE

Mangle is made of many different pieces. Try using a ruler when sketching his framework to capture the stiff, mechanical angles of his body.

1 Sketch Mangle's frame. His heads are very different shapes: the Foxy-style head is bottle shaped and the exposed endoskeleton head is a thick T shape.

2 Begin adding form to your drawing. Instead of ovals, his body is made up of straight lines, with large circles around his major joints.

3

Sketch two teardrop shapes to create Mangle's ears, then use your guidelines to outline his hands and feet. Notice that his exposed endoskeleton foot is square in shape, while his other feet are rounded.

4

Stack cylinders to form Mangle's fingers. Draw a small, neat circle for his tail and connect it to his robotic leg. Mark the shape of his snout, jaw, and fur on the Foxy-style face, and a wide eye and rounded teeth on the exposed face. Don't forget his bow tie!

5

Outline Mangle's eyes, noses, and lipstick. Pointed cones create his sharp teeth. His endoskeleton can be tricky to draw. Carefully pencil in rectangles, cubes, and circles around his frame, curving the shapes with the angle of his limbs.

6

Wavy lines create Mangle's loose wires. Carefully mark their placement, then firm up your lines when you're happy with how they look. Add eyelids and red cheeks.

7

Solidify your outline and erase any remaining guidelines. It should look as if Mangle is reaching toward you. Remember: fingers aren't perfectly straight: they curve and bend around the knuckles.

ART TIP

Mangle may be a damaged mess of parts, but his robotic body is precise, so keep your lines neat.

8

Darkly shade Mangle's wires, ankle joints, eye sockets, and open mouth. Add a series of short, sharp lines to your drawing to capture his shiny but dented metal structure.

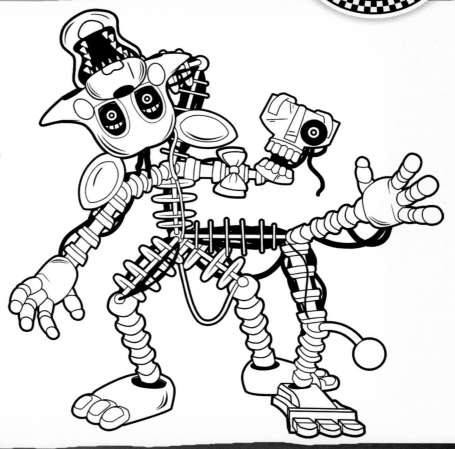

SPRINGTRAP

Springtrap is a hybrid animatronic/springlock suit. He has five fingers and his eyes are set in his head. He thrives on fear, so place your lines with confidence.

1 Pencil in Springtrap's frame. His body is badly damaged, so his head should droop down and his stance should be wide to show the weight of his limbs.

2 Flesh out his body. His wedge-shaped feet are positioned at different angles. This causes one to look wider and thicker, while the other is long and thin.

3

Mark Springtrap's fingers. Unlike the other animatronics, he has five fingers. Position his ears and outline the shape of his snout.

4

Use your guides to continue adding detail. A thin crescent creates his wide, menacing grin. Short, sharp lines create his eyelids.

ART TIP

Follow your construction lines. For these characters, the eyeline should pass through the center of the eye.

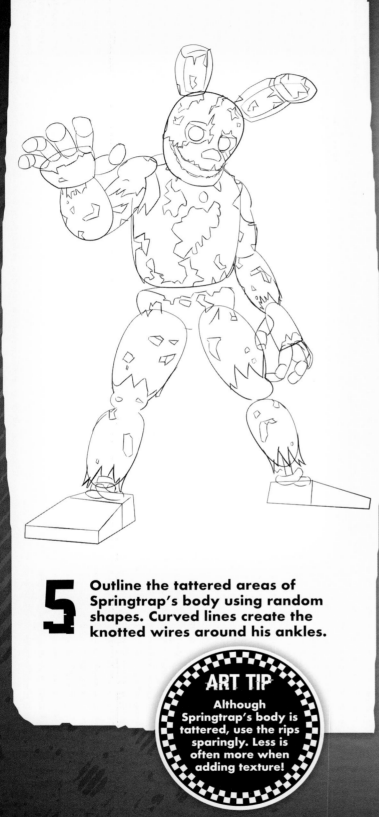

6 Add detail to your drawing. Three long triangles define his toes. Add his exposed wires, curling out of his right ear and body where the suit splits open. Draw his square teeth.

5 Outline the tattered areas of Springtrap's body using random shapes. Curved lines create the knotted wires around his ankles.

ART TIP

Although Springtrap's body is tattered, use the rips sparingly. Less is often more when adding texture!

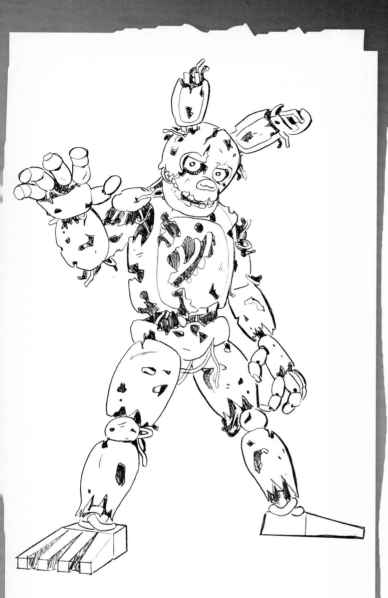

8 Finish shading. Springtrap's eyes look more human than the other cast members'. Take care when shading around them to create a sense of depth in the suit.

7 Erase any rough lines. Shade the darkest areas of your drawing. Because Springtrap's suit has deteriorated, don't worry about keeping your lines neat.

BALLOON BOY

To give this curious animatronic his balloon-like shape, the stripes on his shirt should closely follow the curve of his body.

1

Pencil in Balloon Boy's framework. His head is large and his body is small. Notice how his legs are bent and his right arm is stretched high.

2

Add shape to BB's body. We're looking up at him here, so the soles of his feet are large and flat, his torso round, and his legs short and squat.

ART TIP

Using a compass will help to give BB's round body and balloons a smooth and precise look.

3

Sketch large eyes, rosy cheeks, and a cone nose. Mark the base of his cap and two buttons on his shirt.

4

Draw three large circles. Stretch lines from each balloon's center to BB's hand. Use a rectangle for his sign.

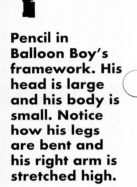

5 Continue adding shape to the balloons and sign. Teardrop shapes create his hat's propeller. Pencil in his hair and draw his wide grin.

6 Begin to define BB's bright eyes and draw his wide, square teeth. Add stripes to his hat and shirt, and detail his buttons.

7 Neatly write "Balloons!" on BB's sign and add curved lines to the balloons. Shade the darkest areas and erase any remaining guidelines.

8 Outline BB, keeping the curved lines on his hat and shirt light. Thick black around his eyes and in his mouth will make his expression pop!

MARIONETTE

The Marionette (also known as the Puppet) is slender and much taller than the other animatronics. No matter the figure's build, their base skeleton remains the same.

1

Pencil in the Marionette's framework. Use long lines for his tall figure, with a slim pelvic shape and raised left leg. His head isn't a perfect circle.

2

Add shape to your drawing. To capture his slender build, keep the outline close to his frame. The Marionette doesn't have feet, so his legs should come to thin points.

3

Define the shape of his mask and draw his upper eyelids and broad grin. Pencil the buttons on his chest.

4

Add three long, curled fingers to each hand. Draw a series of tightly curved lines on his limbs. Finish shaping his eyes and add a circle for his cheek.

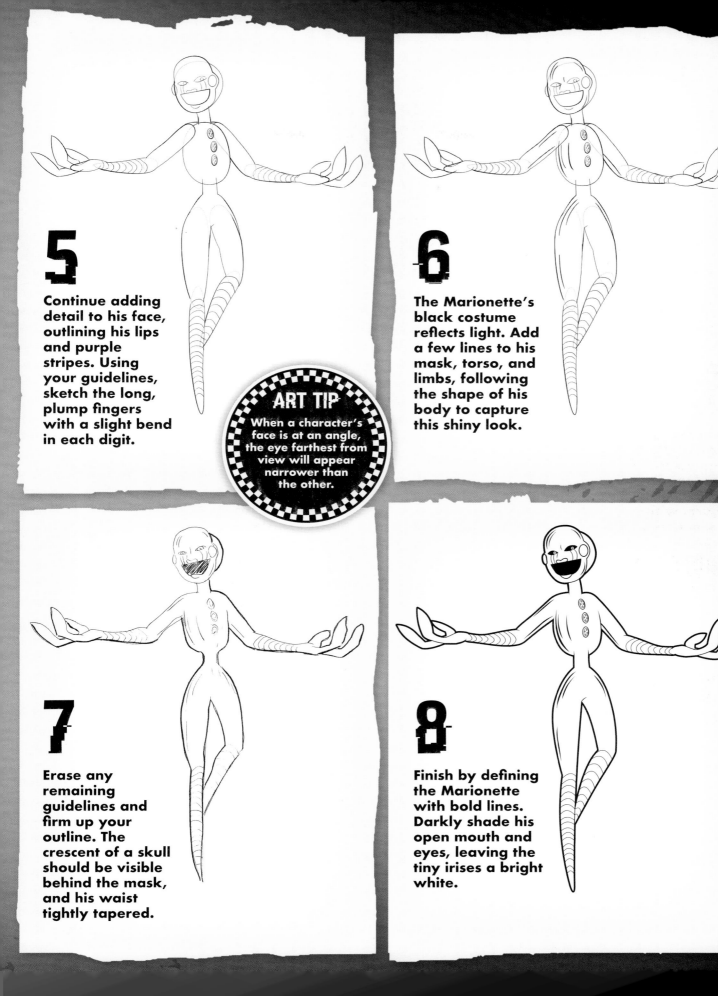

5

Continue adding detail to his face, outlining his lips and purple stripes. Using your guidelines, sketch the long, plump fingers with a slight bend in each digit.

6

The Marionette's black costume reflects light. Add a few lines to his mask, torso, and limbs, following the shape of his body to capture this shiny look.

ART TIP

When a character's face is at an angle, the eye farthest from view will appear narrower than the other.

7

Erase any remaining guidelines and firm up your outline. The crescent of a skull should be visible behind the mask, and his waist tightly tapered.

8

Finish by defining the Marionette with bold lines. Darkly shade his open mouth and eyes, leaving the tiny irises a bright white.

NIGHTMARE BONNIE

Nightmare Bonnie is much taller than the original Bonnie. In this drawing, his hunched stance will help to show his height.

1 Sketch Nightmare Bonnie's framework. Emphasize the curve in his spine and bent knees to portray his bulky build.

2 Add shape to your frame using wide ovals for his limbs. Notice that his feet are different shapes, with a wedge forming his exposed left foot.

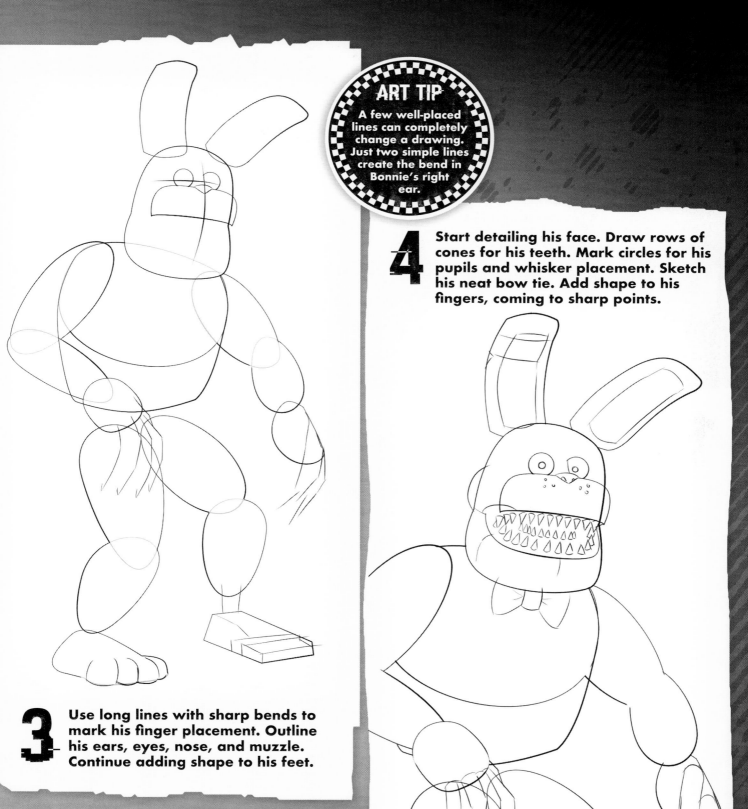

ART TIP

A few well-placed lines can completely change a drawing. Just two simple lines create the bend in Bonnie's right ear.

4 Start detailing his face. Draw rows of cones for his teeth. Mark circles for his pupils and whisker placement. Sketch his neat bow tie. Add shape to his fingers, coming to sharp points.

3 Use long lines with sharp bends to mark his finger placement. Outline his ears, eyes, nose, and muzzle. Continue adding shape to his feet.

5 Have fun outlining the deteriorated areas on Nightmare Bonnie's suit, using random, jagged lines. He has a large tear in his torso and damage around his eyes.

6 Use your base guidelines to sketch his visible endoskeleton, including his spine and knees. Draw loose wires, wiry whiskers, and light lines on his eyes.

7 Define his mechanical fingers and sharp nails. Erase any remaining guidelines and begin shading the rips and tears on Bonnie's body.

8 Add thick, dark shading to your drawing. Finalize your pencil work, keeping your outline rough to give him a damaged appearance.

NIGHTMARE CHICA

Nightmare Chica's beak is much larger than original Chica's: all the better to eat with.

1 Lightly pencil in Nightmare Chica's frame. Notice how she is slouched forward. Keep her head long and slim. This will help to place her open beak.

2 Add shape to her body. Although Nightmare Chica has a broad build, her body isn't as round as her original counterpart's.

3

Outline Chica's rounded torso. Use your guidelines to place her facial features, curving her puffy cheeks outward. Mark her fingers and the shape of her toes. Draw three slim ovals to create her tuft of hair.

ART TIP

Leave space between Chica's upper and lower jaw. Her upper beak has a gradual curve with sharp points, extending from her cheeks. The lower half is a wide, flat oval.

4

Add a plate to Chica's hand. Sketch Nightmare Cupcake, beginning with a large circle for his head. Add his base, two eyes, and a lit candle.

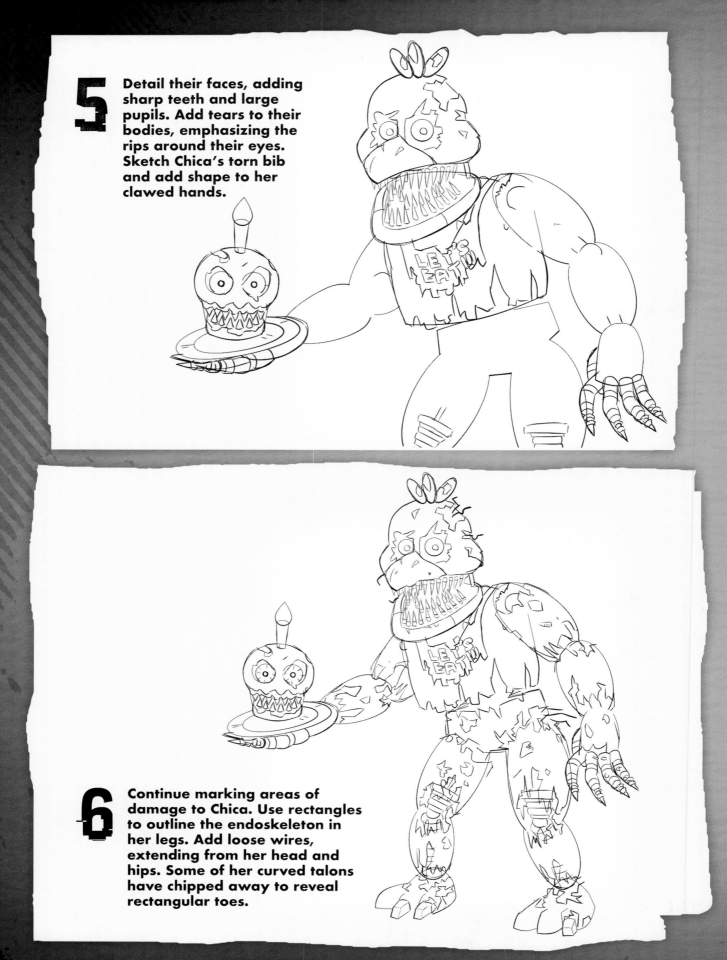

5 Detail their faces, adding sharp teeth and large pupils. Add tears to their bodies, emphasizing the rips around their eyes. Sketch Chica's torn bib and add shape to her clawed hands.

6 Continue marking areas of damage to Chica. Use rectangles to outline the endoskeleton in her legs. Add loose wires, extending from her head and hips. Some of her curved talons have chipped away to reveal rectangular toes.

7 Begin adding value to the darkest areas of Chica and Nightmare Cupcake. This will add depth to your drawing, giving it a 3D look.

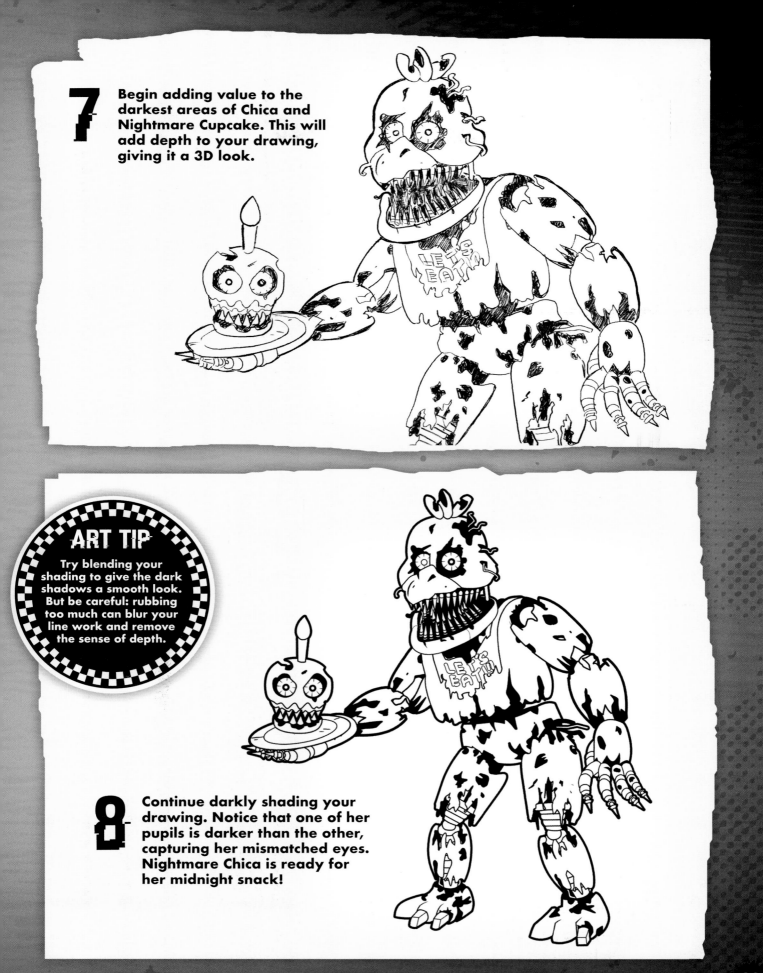

ART TIP

Try blending your shading to give the dark shadows a smooth look. But be careful: rubbing too much can blur your line work and remove the sense of depth.

8 Continue darkly shading your drawing. Notice that one of her pupils is darker than the other, capturing her mismatched eyes. Nightmare Chica is ready for her midnight snack!

NIGHTMARE FREDBEAR

Without his top hat and bow tie, this Fredbear would be unrecognizable! Use clean lines for his accessories to contrast his scary damaged figure.

1 Create Nightmare Fredbear's frame. He is looking straight at us. Curve his arms outward and keep his stance wide to support his large build.

2 Begin adding shape to his body, using squat circles and ovals. Since we will see his exposed ankles, the ovals forming his calves don't stretch all the way to his feet.

3

Outline Fredbear's top hat and ears. Use your guidelines to add his muzzle. Emphasize the shape of his cheeks and draw his gaping jaw. Mark the placement of his long fingers.

4

Continue adding shape to his body, with your lines tapering in tightly around his joints. Large crescents form his fingers. Outline his belly and sketch his bow tie and buttons. Draw two small eyes.

5

Draw two rows of long, sharp teeth in Fredbear's open mouth. Add a further row along his belly. Sketch exposed wires around his face and ears. Use your base framework to outline his endoskeleton.

ART TIP

Don't be afraid to exaggerate Fredbear's jaw. The bigger the head is in proportion to the body, the more weighty and monstrous the character will appear.

6

Pencil in the rips on his fur. There are distinct tears around his eyes and mouth, exposing his dark gums. Add light lines around his eyes to create a bloodshot effect.

7

Thicken the loose wires around his head. Add a row of small circles to create the screws along his gums. Define the sections of his fingers using cylinders and sharp-tipped cones.

8

Solidify your outline, capturing Fredbear's furry texture. Add dark shading to the rips on his body. Keep the detail lines on his face light. This contrast between light and heavy lines will create more impact.

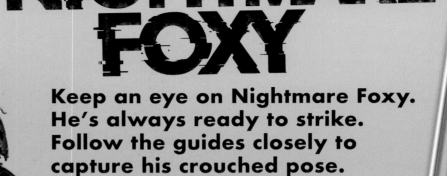

NIGHTMARE FOXY

Keep an eye on Nightmare Foxy. He's always ready to strike. Follow the guides closely to capture his crouched pose.

1 Begin by lightly sketching Nightmare Foxy's framework. Notice that his upper right arm appears much shorter than his upper left arm. This is due to perspective.

2 Add shape to his body and wedge-shaped feet. Take your time: getting his shape and proportions correct now is better than reworking your finished drawing.

3

Outline Foxy's ears, square nose, and tongue. A long semicircle forms his cheek and muzzle. Sketch his cylindrical lower legs and his hooked hand.

4

Continue fleshing out Foxy's face. Sketch the wide tears in the material above his eyes. Mark the placement of his fingers, paying attention to how they bend.

5

Begin detailing your drawing, sketching the tattered sections of Foxy's plates. Stack curved lines to form his bare endoskeleton legs. Draw cones for his claws and teeth.

6

Use short, jagged lines to create Foxy's loose wires. Pencil in the metal frame on his muzzle, curving the lines with the shape of his snout. Add definition to his mechanical feet and fingers.

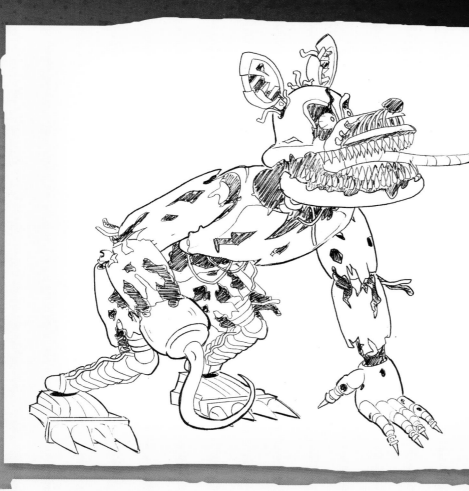

ART TIP

Perspective impacts the sections of Foxy's legs. They are squarer than the typical endoskeleton cylinders. The sections on his right leg will appear slimmer than those on his left.

7

Erase any rough line work and refine your outline. Add final details, including the lines on the base of his hook and rips on his hand, then begin shading.

8

Finish by adding thick black shading to the darkest areas of your drawing. Gripping the pencil close to its tip will create heavy strokes. Contrasting the black of his eye sockets with the clean white of his eyes will help create his menacing stare.

NIGHTMARE BALLOON BOY

This drawing will challenge perspective and proportions as he reaches up toward you. Take care not to get too close when adding his razor-sharp teeth!

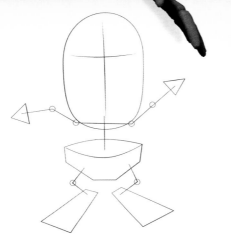

1

Sketch the framework. Keep his limbs short to create the illusion that he is looking up. Draw a long oval for his head to capture his open jaw.

2

Add shape to your sketch, overlapping ovals to create his arms and legs. Draw his eyes, a cone nose, and a curved line for his upper lip.

3

Draw long lines with sharp angles to form his bony fingers. Use your own hand as a reference, looking at how fingers bend and stretch.

4

Flesh out his fingers. Circles create his buttons, eyes, and cheeks. Outline the curve of his cap and add the propeller using teardrop shapes.

5 Add stripes to his outfit, the lines curving with the shape of his body and head. Pencil in his hair and a large semicircle in his open jaw.

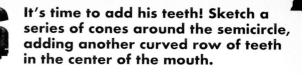

6 It's time to add his teeth! Sketch a series of cones around the semicircle, adding another curved row of teeth in the center of the mouth.

7 Draw his pants, emphasizing the bend in his knees. Add detail to his buttons. Add another circle to his eyes, making them wide and scary.

8 Erase any remaining guidelines then firm up your linework. Shade the inside of his mouth and buttons using heavy pencil strokes.

NIGHTMARE MANGLE

Keep your closet door tightly shut: it's where Nightmare Mangle likes to hide! Experiment with the placement of his reaching limbs.

1 Sketch a large rectangle to outline the closet door, using a ruler to keep your lines straight. The door is at an angle, with the bottom line at a slight diagonal.

2 Sketch Mangle's visible framework, his limbs stretching in different directions. Add shape to the limbs, varying their length but keeping the width consistent to create depth.

ART TIP

If you are struggling with proportions, it can be helpful to think about the unseen parts of a drawing. Consider what Mangle's body looks like behind the door.

4 Thicken the doorframe. Mark his fingers, with one hand wrapping around the door. Pencil in joints and a U shape in his open mouth for his second row of teeth.

3 Continue adding shape to your drawing, penciling in Mangle's square hands and foot. Sketch his muzzle and ears. Outline each head's gaping jaw.

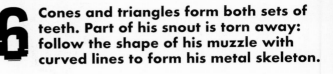

Cones and triangles form both sets of teeth. Part of his snout is torn away: follow the shape of his muzzle with curved lines to form his metal skeleton.

5 Continue placing Mangle's facial features. Use curved lines, cubes, and rectangles to form his endoskeleton, with sharp cones for his claws.

7

Add detail to Mangle's second face, including his eye, triangle nose, and pointed teeth. Mark the knuckles on his fingers. Pencil in a mess of wires, using a mix of short, rough lines and longer, looping lines.

ART TIP

There are lots of fine lines on Mangle's robotic body. Be sure to make your drawing big: the smaller your character, the harder it is to add detail.

8

Begin firming up your drawing and erase any rough work. Add light detail lines to his endoskeleton, keeping them neat and aligned. Mark the areas you will be shading.

9

Finish with heavy shading. Contrast the darkness of the doorway with the shiny metal of Mangle's body. Begin shading at the top and work your way down to avoid smudging pencil onto the clean areas of your drawing.

BALLORA

Ballora loves to dance! Keep your lines loose in this drawing to reflect her flowing ballerina's pose.

1

Create Ballora's outstretched frame. Her upper body bends softly while her right knee has a sharp bend. Her left leg should be long and straight.

2

Flesh out your drawing, using slim ovals. Outline Ballora's chest, following the curve of her spine as she looks up toward the sky.

3

Define her cheeks and then pencil in her eyes, mouth, ear, and hairline. Mark her long fingers with slight curves at their tips. Add her stomach plates.

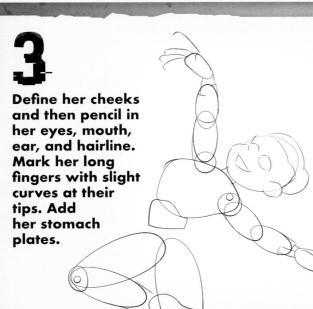

4

Use soft, wavy lines to create her short tutu. Lightly sketch crosshatched lines on her calves and pencil the shape of her shoes, closely following the arch of her foot.

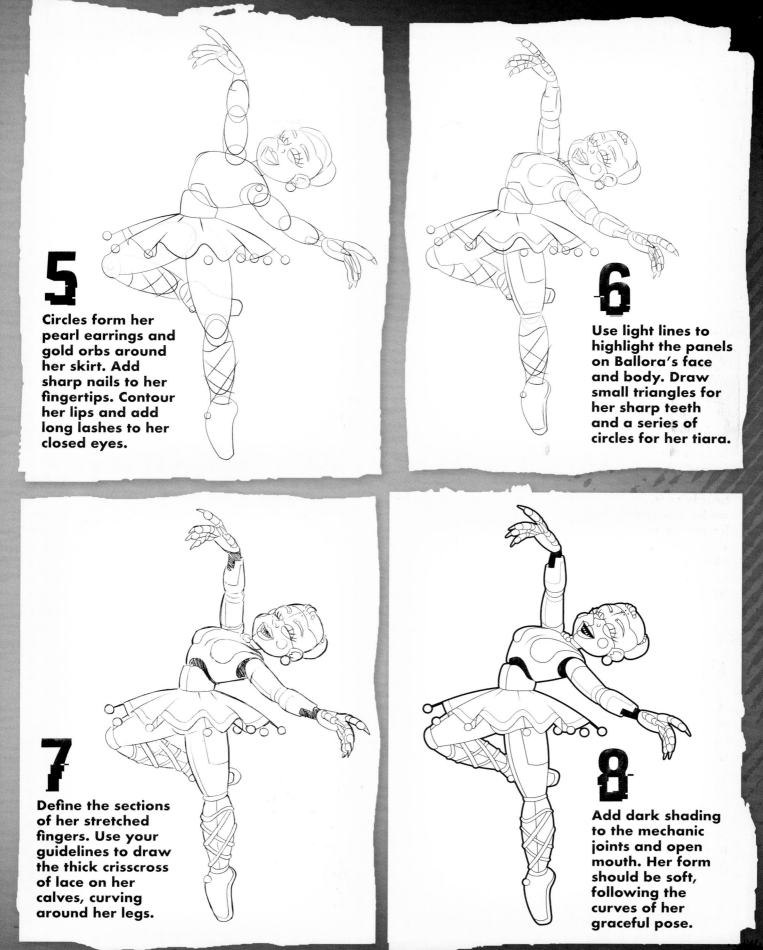

5

Circles form her pearl earrings and gold orbs around her skirt. Add sharp nails to her fingertips. Contour her lips and add long lashes to her closed eyes.

6

Use light lines to highlight the panels on Ballora's face and body. Draw small triangles for her sharp teeth and a series of circles for her tiara.

7

Define the sections of her stretched fingers. Use your guidelines to draw the thick crisscross of lace on her calves, curving around her legs.

8

Add dark shading to the mechanic joints and open mouth. Her form should be soft, following the curves of her graceful pose.

FUNTIME CHICA

Don't let Funtime Chica and Mr. Cupcake fool you: there's a vicious bite beneath their grins. Triangles create sharp teeth.

1

Draw Funtime Chica's frame. Notice the curve in her spine as she tilts forward and that her toes point inward. Keep her arms angled and outstretched to hold Mr. Cupcake.

2

Add a series of ovals to flesh out your figure. Although her right arm will be covered by her torso, it's useful to sketch the full limb to correctly capture the proportions.

3

Firm up your outline. Funtime Chica's figure is more humanlike than her original counterpart, with her face and torso being slimmer and curvier. Shape her eyes, beak, and feather tuft.

4

Sketch an oval to create a plate. Draw Mr. Cupcake's outline, starting with a large circle. Add the lit candle and eyes.

5

Start detailing your drawing. Add lipstick to Chica's beak, and large needle teeth to the characters' mouths. Lightly mark her paneling, joints, and speaker.

6

Continue highlighting the mechanical sections on Chica's hands, face, and body. Draw her long eyelashes and rosy cheeks. Add stripes to Mr. Cupcake's candle.

7

Tidy your line work and erase any guidelines. Begin adding value to the darkest areas of your drawing, using short strokes to layer on the shading.

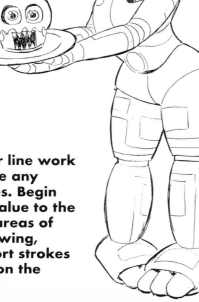

8

Finish your drawing with thick black lines. Keep the interior panel and hinge lines light and crisp for a clean robotic look. Funtime Chica is ready for her close-up!

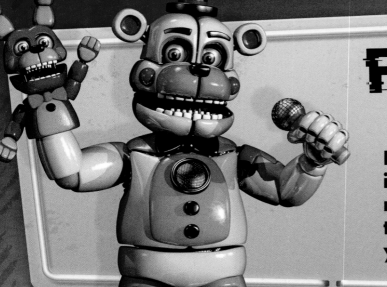

FUNTIME FREDDY

Funtime Freddy likes introducing Bon-Bon to his new friends! Exaggerate their expressions to give your drawing character.

1

Pencil Funtime Freddy's frame. Exaggerate the bends in his arms, carefully marking his joints. Add guidelines to his face, keeping the direction of his gaze in mind.

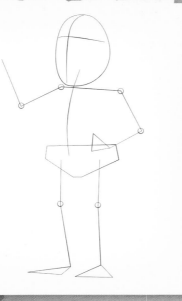

2

Build upon your frame, adding shape to Freddy's body: ovals for his limbs and circles for his elbows and knees. Notice that his feet are at slightly different angles.

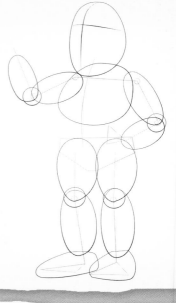

3

Using your guidelines, add Freddy's facial features and top hat. Outline his bow tie and the speaker on his chest. Place his fingers, as if curled around something.

4

Add the microphone to Freddy's left hand. Sketch Bon-Bon's framework where Freddy's right hand would be.

5

Add shape to
Bon-Bon's arms
and ears, and
sketch his facial
features. Add
detail to Freddy's
face and buttons
to his shirt. Draw
four cylinders on
each foot for his
toes and flesh
out his fingers.

6

Use light lines to
create Freddy's
paneling. Add
detail to both
characters,
including big,
toothy smiles.
Draw a spiked
line where
Bon-Bon bops
Freddy's nose.

7

Tidy up your
linework. Erase
any rough
markings.
Begin shading
your drawing,
adding bright
highlights to
Freddy's hat
and buttons.

8

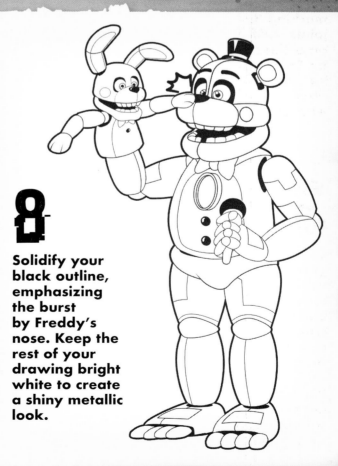

Solidify your
black outline,
emphasizing
the burst
by Freddy's
nose. Keep the
rest of your
drawing bright
white to create
a shiny metallic
look.

FUNTIME FOXY

The Funtime crew are in better condition than their original counterparts. Avoid scuffing their plates by using an eraser to keep your drawing clean!

1

Sketch Funtime Foxy's frame, carefully following the reference to capture the angled pose. Keep your pencil strokes light as you draw a long, wide S shape for Foxy's tail.

2

Keep your ovals close to Foxy's outline to portray their slim build. Although their legs are straight, there should still be a slight indent around the knees.

3

Use two tear shapes for Foxy's ears and a curved rectangle for their long snout. Sketch the bow tie, speaker, and fingers. Follow your guideline to draw their bushy tail.

4

Define Foxy's jaw, adding a small rectangular nose. Draw a small tuft of hair between the ears. Add shape to the fingers.

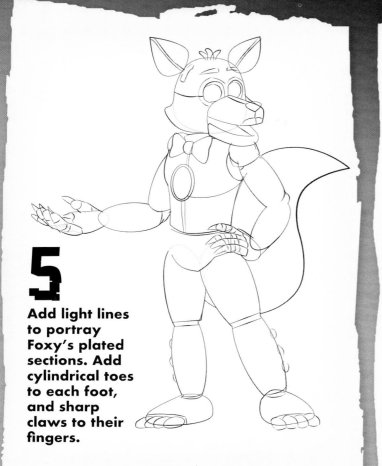

5

Add light lines to portray Foxy's plated sections. Add cylindrical toes to each foot, and sharp claws to their fingers.

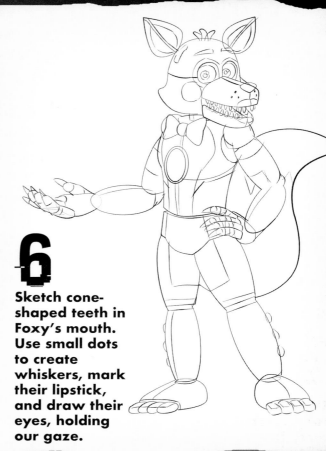

6

Sketch cone-shaped teeth in Foxy's mouth. Use small dots to create whiskers, mark their lipstick, and draw their eyes, holding our gaze.

7

Erase any remaining guidelines and firm up your line work. Add shading to Foxy's joints and robotic features.

8

Gradually layer thick black onto the darkest areas to add depth to your drawing, giving the shadows a smooth look.

TWISTED FREDDY

Twisted Freddy is truly frightening! Contrast the soft bubbles of his boils with the sharp points of his claws and many sets of teeth.

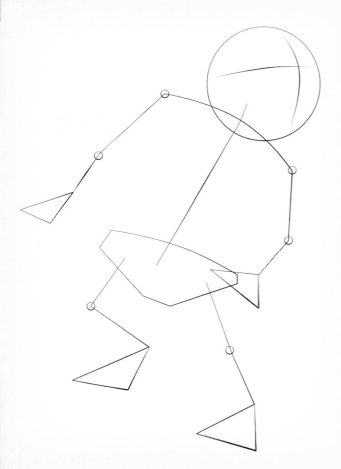

1 Begin by sketching Twisted Freddy's framework, capturing his leaning pose. The base shape for this Freddy's head is a neat, round circle.

2 Use squat circles and ovals to add shape to his body. The right side of his torso curves out more than the left due to his twisted stance.

3

Use your guides to place Freddy's muzzle and ears. Extend the outline of his jaw down, overlapping his torso. Mark his long fingers and add shape to his feet.

4

Outline his huge eyes and draw his top hat. Add his teeth, then continue using cones to add shape to his fingers and clawed feet. Mark zigzag lines in the center of his stomach.

5

Layer circles to create his cold gaze. When sketching his teeth, vary the size and direction of each cone to create a rough, jagged look. Use random lines to create tears around his mouth, revealing his gums.

6

Add the boils to his body. Vary the circles in size and shape. The clusters of boils should follow Freddy's outline around his right shoulder and cheek. Add round screws to the exposed metal around his stomach.

ART TIP

Twisted Freddy is covered in boils, but you don't need to draw lots of them. Drawing small patches of boils is a more effective way to create the look.

Begin firming up your line work. Add light, curved lines to a handful of the boils to make them appear as if they are filled with fluid.

8

Solidify your outline. Three simple lines will give his top hat a 3D look. Darkly shade around Freddy's eyes, mouth, exposed kneecap, and sharp-toothed hole in his belly.

TWISTED FOXY

Even when stuck in the ground, Foxy is dangerous. His outstretched arms make it seem as if he is trying the heave himself out of the dirt.

1 Sketch Twisted Foxy's framework. Use a large oval for his face and place the eyeline high on his head. His limbs are long. As his legs are buried, a semicircle forms his pelvic outline.

2 Use ovals to form the shape of his arms and circles to mark his shoulders. Although his chest is wide, his stomach should curve inward to capture his slim build.

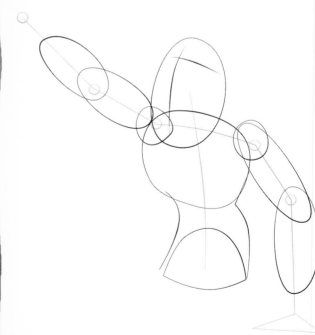

3

Mark Foxy's hook and his wide, square fingers on his left hand. Using your guides, outline his open jaw. Sketch his nose and ears, with a small gap between his left ear and his head. Use straight, sharp lines to outline the ground around him.

4

Add shape to his hook, using wavy lines around its base. Curved lines create his cheek and extended brow. Connect his ear to his head. A cylinder forms his left arm.

ART TIP

Exaggerate the curved lines of Twisted Foxy's claws to give them a frightening look. They are hooked, unlike the other animatronics' cone-shaped claws.

5

Shape his claws. Begin adding detail, sketching small bumps on his body. Draw the rips on his face, sketching lines at the edge of his open mouth. Shape the dirt around him with some pieces of earth in the air to create the illusion he has just burst out of the ground.

6

Draw his visible eye and sketch his teeth. Pencil in the wires around his head and shoulders. Continue adding rough circles to form the fungal growth on his body. Add light lines to his chest and stomach, emphasizing his scrawny build.

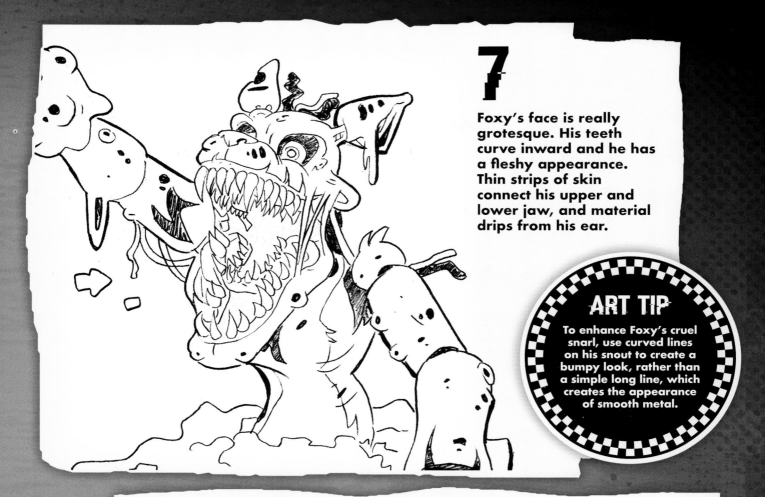

7

Foxy's face is really grotesque. His teeth curve inward and he has a fleshy appearance. Thin strips of skin connect his upper and lower jaw, and material drips from his ear.

ART TIP

To enhance Foxy's cruel snarl, use curved lines on his snout to create a bumpy look, rather than a simple long line, which creates the appearance of smooth metal.

8

Firm up your pencil work and erase any guidelines. Add dark shading to Foxy's rips, eye sockets, and mouth. Lightly pencil in random lines on the dirt to give it an uneven texture.

TWISTED CHICA

Twisted Chica is on the hunt. There are lots of overlapping lines in this drawing. Take your time to ensure her proportions are correct.

1 Sketch Twisted Chica's frame. As she is leaning forward to roar, her head should be large and egg shaped. Draw a circle for Twisted Cupcake, connecting to Chica's head and shoulder.

2 Begin adding shape to her body. Her stomping stance will challenge perspective. Pay close attention to the reference drawing to help ensure the angles are right.

ART TIP

Twisted Chica's feet are similar to those of a real chicken. It can be helpful to think of talons like regular fingers: consider their joint placement and how they bend.

3

Continue shaping her body. Though her limbs are broad, they should taper in around her joints. Draw a teardrop shape to outline the main portion of her beak. Sketch a rough semicircle on her hip and draw candles on both Cupcakes.

4

Mark her curled fingers and outline her right kneecap. Build the shape of her upper jaw around her beak and add her thick tufts of hair. Draw the upper Cupcake's jagged outline and add flames to both candles, which are more exaggerated than their other counterparts.

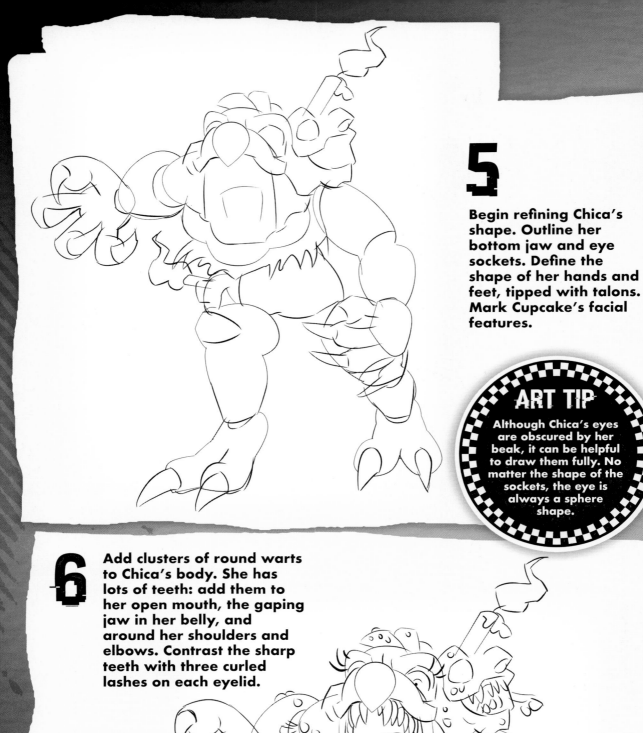

5

Begin refining Chica's shape. Outline her bottom jaw and eye sockets. Define the shape of her hands and feet, tipped with talons. Mark Cupcake's facial features.

ART TIP

Although Chica's eyes are obscured by her beak, it can be helpful to draw them fully. No matter the shape of the sockets, the eye is always a sphere shape.

6

Add clusters of round warts to Chica's body. She has lots of teeth: add them to her open mouth, the gaping jaw in her belly, and around her shoulders and elbows. Contrast the sharp teeth with three curled lashes on each eyelid.

7

Begin refining your line work. Detail your drawing, adding curved lines to her arms and legs, as well as her talons and the teeth in her belly. This is a simple way to create a textured look. Define Cupcake's facial features.

8

Add a thick outline and darkly shade Twisted Chica's open mouths. Take care with the lines around Twisted Cupcake on her shoulder. It should look as if it has merged with her body.

TWISTED WOLF

Part wolf, part machine, Twisted Wolf is one of Afton's most terrifying creations. Have fun contrasting the different textures on his body.

1 Lightly draw Twisted Wolf's framework. Capture his open, howling pose keeping his stance wide, arms angled, and face tilted upward. Don't forget a curved line for his tail!

2 Begin fleshing out your drawing. Although he is part wolf, his body's proportions are similar to those of a human. Notice the exaggerated curve in his right ankle.

3

Continue adding shape to his body, outlining his feet and tail. Mark his curled fingers. Sketch his ear and open jowls. A diagonal line from the top of his head to the top of his shoulder creates his long neck.

4

Pencil in his robotic elements: triangular spikes on his arm, rows of cone-shaped teeth, the panels on his leg, and exposed endoskeleton. Contrast a robotic left hand and foot with a clawed wolfish right hand and foot.

5

Continue adding detail to the Wolf's body. Add an angry eye to the triangular socket. Draw his fur in sections, falling in different directions to give it a realistic look. Rough circles and lines add texture to his robotic limbs.

6

Lightly draw a series of rectangles around the Wolf's body, with a few of them overlapping. These lines do not have to be neat to capture their glitchy look.

7

Erase any rough line work and begin firming up your outline. Contrast loose, rough strokes for the Wolf's fur with neat, clean lines for his mechanical body parts.

8

Shade the darkest areas of your drawing, ensuring his teeth are a bright white to give them a vicious look against the dark background. Twisted Wolf is ready to do your bidding.

GLAMROCK CHICA

Glamrock Chica is the star of the show with her guitar! Begin with an A shape when drawing a five-point star.

1

Start by sketching her frame. Take care when placing her limbs: the proportions might appear warped due to her seated position.

2

Flesh out the figure. As her legs are at an angle, use wide ovals for her lower limbs. Add a line to mark her guitar's placement.

3

Start adding detail. Triangles form the basis of Chica's bow, earrings, toes, and shoulder pads. Leave her beak wide open.

4

Draw the guitar's star-shaped body, a long rectangle for the neck, and a rough triangle for the head. Use a ruler for clean lines.

5 Simple shapes create the guitar's detail. Draw a small layer of fabric on each side of her bow, and give the earrings a 3D effect.

6 Continue adding detail: six round teeth, strokes of blusher, long lashes, and big eyes. Draw her feathered hair, falling in curved sections.

7 Begin shading your drawing. A pattern can make clothing more dynamic. Have fun decorating Chica's pants with spots and stripes!

8 Firm up your line work and use heavy shading around Chica's eyes, mouth, and pants. You're ready to rock!

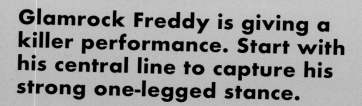

GLAMROCK FREDDY

Glamrock Freddy is giving a killer performance. Start with his central line to capture his strong one-legged stance.

1 Sketch Glamrock Freddy's framework. He's ready to put on a show, so his pose is really dynamic with dramatic bends in his limbs.

2 Flesh out your drawing. Glamrock Freddy is slightly slimmer than the other Freddy animatronics. Keep your ovals long and slim. The angle of his left arm will make the limbs appear shorter.

3

Using your base sketch, start defining Freddy's shape. His open jaw is almost a mirror image of the top half of his head. Pencil in his bow tie and shoulder pads.

4

A cube with rounded corners forms Freddy's top hat. Draw a long, slim cylinder to create his microphone stand, with his left hand wrapping around it. The microphone is also made of cylinders.

ART TIP

Freddy's hand forms a rock 'n' roll gesture. Practice drawing hands in different poses. No matter the hand's position, finger sizes always stay the same.

5 Add detail to Freddy's face, open in a wide smile. Shape his bracelets and decorate with small circles to form studs and add an earring. Mark his claws and the pads on his raised foot. Stack cylinders to form his fingers.

6 Sharp-tipped triangles form his teeth and fingernails. Outline his face paint and sketch the lightning bolt on his chest. Pencil in panels on his leg and torso.

7

Draw an oval to create the microphone stand's base. Erase your rough linework. You should now have a clear drawing of Glamrock Freddy.

ART TIP

Contrasting light line work for detail with a thick outline and dark shading will add depth to your drawing. Move your pencil in an even motion when shading.

8

Before Freddy takes to the stage, solidify your drawing with heavy blacks and darkly shade his mechanic joints and microphone.

ROXANNE WOLF

Roxanne Wolf is always ready to rock out on stage! Contrast her curvy pose with the hard, straight angles of her keytar.

1 Draw Roxanne Wolf's framework, paying close attention to her pose. Notice that her knees turn inward and her head is slightly tilted.

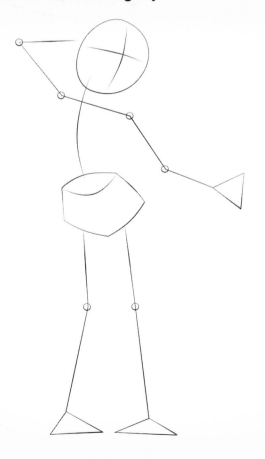

2 Add shape to her body, using slim cylinders for her arms and curved teardrop shapes for her legs.

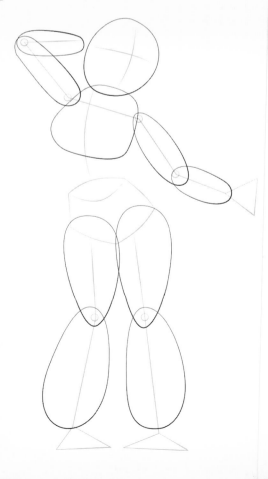

3 Pencil in Roxanne's hair and tail. Be sure to draw their full shape. Place her facial features and ear. Draw the central line for her keytar.

4 The keytar looks very angular, but can be broken down into simple cuboids and rectangles. Use a ruler to keep your lines neat.

6 Sketch her accessories while also marking her panels and articulated joints by her ear and left arm. Add shape to her hair, falling in sections rather than individual strands.

5 Begin firming up her outline, adding her belt and shoulder pads. Draw her mouth in a wide friendly grin. A simple line across her left eye will show it is shut in a wink.

ART TIP

When wrapping a design around a body part, such as Roxanne's belt or stripes, begin by identifying the base curve of the pattern before adding detail.

Use thick blacks to shade the darkest areas of your drawing. Ensure there's a bright sparkle in her open eye to capture her mischievous nature.

7 Erase any rough line work. Use light lines to add sections to Roxanne's hair, giving it a textured look. Add value to the pattern on her clothing and keytar, as well as her stripes.

MONTGOMERY GATOR

Punk rockers like Monty know that it's cool to put your unique stamp on creations. Have fun designing his Mohawk and have fun placing his scales.

1 Pencil in Montgomery Gator's frame. His shoulders are close to his chin and his body long, ready to hold his bass guitar. His tail has a light curve.

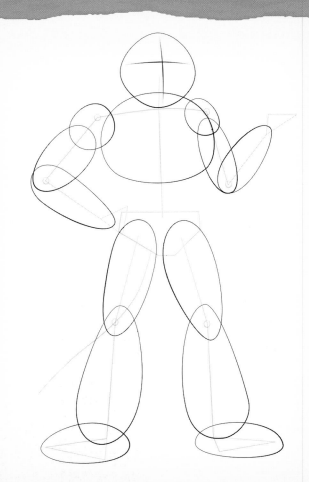

2 Add shape to his limbs, with large circles defining his shoulders. Notice that his legs flair out around the ankles.

3 Sketch the guitar's central line, curling his fingers around it. Use simple shapes to add his shoulder pads and Mohawk. Flesh out his tail and sketch his jawline.

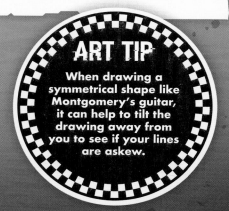

ART TIP

When drawing a symmetrical shape like Montgomery's guitar, it can help to tilt the drawing away from you to see if your lines are askew.

4 Draw Montgomery's star glasses. Use a ruler to lightly pencil in the shape of his guitar. It can be broken down into a series of interlinked rectangles, with a sharp indent at the base of its body.

5 Mark his joints and add shape to his fingers. Outline his bracelets and sketch buttons on his guitar. Define the shape of his snout with a long, thin smile and pencil in his eyelids.

6 Continue detailing your drawing. Add his lightning-bolt face paint, wide eyes, and sharp teeth. Lightly mark patches of scales across his body. Add strings to his guitar.

8 Before Montgomery takes to the stage, add dark shading to your drawing. Contrasting thick blacks with clean white will give your drawing a sharp snap!

7 Refine your pencil work and erase any remaining guidelines. Use rough lines to create sections of hair in his Mohawk. Shade his claws and eye sockets.

ART TIP

When shading claws, move your pencil in the direction of their curve and leave a white highlight. This will show their contoured shape.

HAPPY FROG

Move over, Freddy! Mediocre Melodies' singing frog would kill to be Fazbear Entertainment's next superstar.

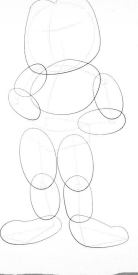

1

Lightly sketch Happy Frog's framework. Her pose is bashful, with her shoulders low and hands behind her back. Draw a large oval for her head.

2

Flesh out your drawing. The outline of her face should be slightly wider than the guideline. A wide M shape forms her brow. Keep the curves soft.

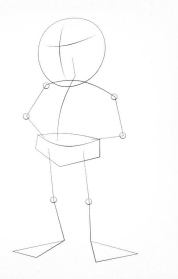

3

Mark her belly and toes. Pencil in her facial features. Her eye sockets aren't perfectly round. Two short curved lines form her nose. Draw a small circle above her head.

4

Keep adding detail to her face. She has long lashes and big eyes. As her head is tilted, the eye farthest from you will not be a full circle. Add her large square teeth.

5

Draw Happy Frog's pupils and connect the orb to her head. Create a ribbed effect on her belly by drawing a series of lines, curving gently with the shape of her body. Define the shape of her feet.

6

Identify her articulated joints, using an oval and small cylinder to visibly connect her shoulder to her torso. Use thin, curved lines to clearly mark the joints around her hips and ankles.

7

Erase any rough marks. Thicken the antenna and begin shading the darkest areas of your drawing. Add short, light lines to create a worn look.

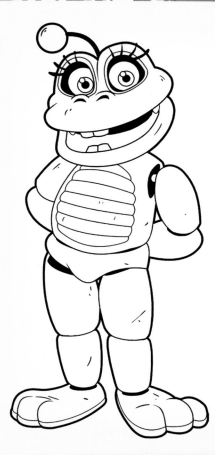

8

Polish your line work and darkly shade Happy Frog's joints, eyes, and mouth. Firm up her eyelashes and antenna. Happy Frog is ready to hop onstage!

MR. HIPPO

Mr. Hippo's expressive face is made up of lots of circles. Let's begin before he starts telling one of his long-winded stories!

1 Sketch Mr. Hippo's framework. His body is at a slight angle. Draw sharp bends in the elbows to capture his open-armed pose.

2 Layer a series of ovals to add shape to his body. Outline his head, extending away from your guides toward the bottom to create a wide, square jaw.

3 Add facial features. His nostrils overlap with his eye sockets. Mark a cross in each ear to find their central point.

4 Form his top hat on the center of his head. Draw a flower on his chest, with slim ovals forming the petals.

5 Add shape to his hands, feet, and body, beginning to highlight the mechanic joints. Draw his eyes, with droopy upper eyelids.

6 Using your guides, draw two small circles in the center of his ears. Sketch his muzzle and square teeth.

7 Begin shading, keeping a bright highlight on his hat to create a 3D look. Add a few scuffs to his body by penciling in some small lines.

8 Erase any remaining guidelines and finish shading the darkest areas of your drawing, highlighting the gleam in his eyes and on his buttons.

PIG PATCH

Pig Patch loves to play banjo riffs. Positioning his feet helps to create his leaning stance. Take your time getting their base shape right.

1

Create Pig Patch's framework. Because his head is tilted upward, use a long oval for his face and place the eyeline high on his head.

2

Add shape to his body, ensuring his torso follows the curve of his spine. Closely follow your guidelines to draw the curve of his toes, capturing his leaning stance.

3

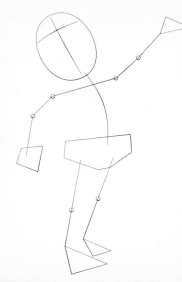

Pig Patch's body should now have clear mechanical sections. Pencil in his facial features, drawing his eyes and snout. Add two large tear shapes for his ears.

4

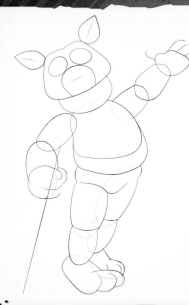

The banjo can be broken down into simple shapes. Two large circles form the body, rectangles form the bridge, and parallel lines connect to a rounded hexagon for the neck and head.

5 Draw two large squares for his teeth. He is looking at a downward angle, so his eyes should sit in lower part of the sockets, as if crossed.

6 Refine Pig Patch's features, sketching his eyes, nostrils, and inner ears. Mark scuffs on his body and add an X to the center of his belly button.

7 Erase any remaining guidelines. Begin shading the darkest areas of your drawing. Use short dashes to create the banjo's bracket hooks.

8 Finish by darkly shading your drawing and firming up your outline. Pig Patch is ready for his big banjo solo.

NEDD BEAR

Nedd Bear might be a bit goofy, but the lines on his tie and electric box are neat, straight, and evenly spaced.

1

Sketch Nedd Bear's frame. Lightly mark his joints. This will help to capture his waving pose. Carefully place the construction lines on his face.

2

Use ovals to add shape to his body. His torso should stretch all the way to the top of his pelvic outline, capturing his small build and round stomach.

3

Clearly define the plated sections of his body. Add two round ears and muzzle. Mark the placement of his fingers and shape his feet. Sketch a cuboid behind his left foot.

4

Begin outlining his facial features and add eight square teeth to his open mouth. Draw a long tie and his small top hat on top of a short zigzag line.

5

Draw his brows and eyeballs. His left eye is a lemon shape and his right eye is circular. Connect him to the electric box with wavy lines creating the wires.

6

Add whiskers and his eyes: his irises and pupils are not perfectly aligned. Add shape to his wrists and hip joints. Thicken the lines around the spring on his head.

7

Outline his tie's pattern with crosshatching. Add value to the darkest areas of your drawing. Lightly mark scratches on Nedd Bear's body.

8

Solidify your outline with thick blacks. Firmly shade his eye sockets, joints, and mouth. Use your lines to create the diamond pattern on his tie.

ORVILLE ELEPHANT

It's Orville's time to shine. A magician never reveals his tricks, but holding your pencil close to the lead will give you more control.

1

Pencil in Orville's framework, extending his right arm high and tilting his head up to capture his enthusiastic pose.

2

Flesh out your drawing. Notice how the ovals forming his bent arm appear shorter and rounder than those on his extended arm. This is due to an artist trick called foreshortening.

3

Continue adding shape to Orville's body. Mark the position of his joints. Sketch his ears and long trunk, which is a big S shape.

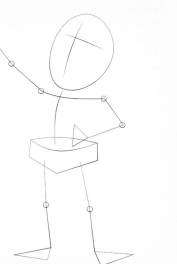

4

It's time to add some magic to your drawing. A tall cylinder forms the top hat's crown, with lines curving around it for the brim. A thin cylinder creates his wand.

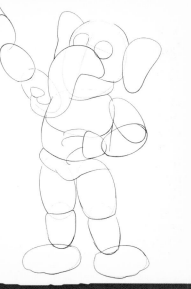

5

Start adding detail to your drawing. Mark his eyebrows and eyes. Define the shape of his feet and outline his toenails with wide ovals.

6

Pencil in his teeth and mark lines around the curve of his trunk to create a wrinkled look. Sketch a flower on his chest, partially hidden by his jaw.

7

Firm up your line work and erase any remaining guidelines. Use short, sharp lines to begin adding depth to Orville's joints, eyes, and mouth.

8

Shade the darkest areas of your drawing. Include a sparkle in his eyes, capturing Orville's eagerness to show off his next trick!

Step-by-step illustrations by Mike Collins and Gethin Wyn Jones
Written by Kirsten Murray
Book design by Amazing15